21st Century Skills Library

HEALTH AT RISK
STEROIDS

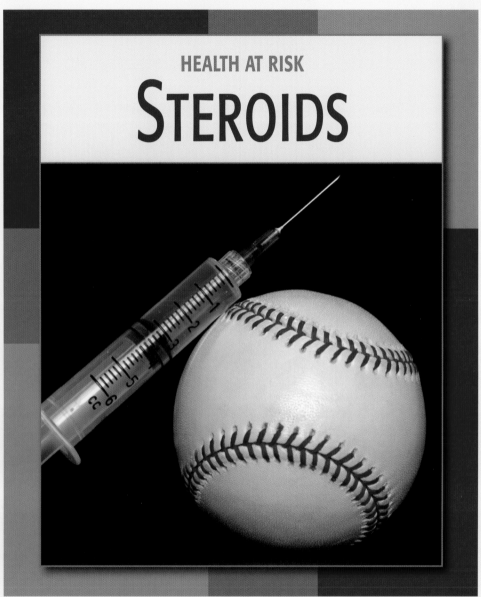

A.R. Schaefer

Cherry Lake Publishing
Ann Arbor, Michigan

Published in the United States of America by Cherry Lake Publishing
Ann Arbor, Michigan
www.cherrylakepublishing.com

Content Advisor: Carolyn Walker, RN, PhD, Professor, School of Nursing, San Diego
State University, San Diego, California

Photo Credits: Cover and page 1, R. Gino Santa Maria/Shutterstock; page 4, Horizon
International Images, Ltd./Alamy; page 7, AP Images/Matt York; page 9, © Mediscan/
Alamy; page 10, © Mediscan/Alamy; page 12, © dan pan/Alamy; page 14, AP Images/
Jason DeCrow; page 16, AP Images/Dieter Endlicher; page 18, AP Images/Laurent
Rebours; page 19, AP Images/Garry L. Jones; page 21, AP Images/Keystone, Laurent
Gillieron; page 22, AP Images/Jeff McIntosh; page 24, AP Images/New Haven Register,
Arnold Gold; page 26, AP Images/Evan Vucci; page 29, AP Images/Mel Evans

Library of Congress Cataloging-in-Publication Data
Schaefer, A.R. (Adam Richard), 1976–
Steroids / A.R. Schaefer.
   p. cm.—(Health at risk)
ISBN-13: 978-1-60279-287-6
ISBN-10: 1-60279-287-9
1. Anabolic steroids—Health aspects—Juvenile literature. 2. Doping in sports—Juvenile
literature. 3. Anabolic steroids—Juvenile literature. I. Title. II. Series.
RC1230.S33 2008
362.29—dc22   2008017502

*Cherry Lake Publishing would like to acknowledge the work of
The Partnership for 21st Century Skills.
Please visit www.21stcenturyskills.org for more information.*

TABLE of CONTENTS

CHAPTER ONE

A Chemical Advantage

Because of its ability to increase muscle size quickly, steroids have been a problem in the sport of weight lifting.

Anabolic steroids are dangerous drugs. They act like male hormones to increase tissue growth. Steroids build muscles quickly, faster than by exercise and lifting weights alone. Steroids also make muscle tissue grow. This helps injuries to muscles heal faster.

Bigger, stronger muscles can help athletes hit a baseball farther or lift heavier weights. They help runners and cyclists go faster and farther. Steroids are used by athletes who aim to break records and earn big paychecks. Millions of ordinary people in the United States and Canada have also taken steroids. They take them to bulk up or improve their game. But when athletes use steroids for extra strength or speed, they gain an unfair advantage over athletes who compete without using drugs. In most sports, using steroids is cheating and against the rules.

Steroids also can cause serious health problems. In most countries, it is illegal to possess or sell steroids

The body makes its own anabolic steroid. It's called testosterone. Testosterone aids muscle growth. It also helps the body recover from intense exercise. The body makes only as much testosterone as it needs. A person who takes steroids has more testosterone than he or she needs. So the body stops making it. When that same person stops taking steroids, the body does not start making more right away. The delay can be months or years. During that time, health can suffer.

without a doctor's prescription. This is the case in the United States and Canada. Athletes don't want to be **disqualified** or fined or jailed. So those who use steroids try to keep it secret. Today's news is full of stories of famous athletes who lose their medals, records, and **reputations** when they are caught.

Major League Baseball player Ken Caminiti was one of the first sports figures to admit publicly that he took steroids. He used them for a few years to boost his strength. He started taking steroids when he injured his shoulder. His injuries healed quickly and his muscle mass increased. He became a more powerful hitter and fielder.

Major league baseball player Ken Caminiti admitted to taking steroids after a shoulder injury. The need to keep playing while injured entices some professional athletes to take steroids.

He even won the Most Valuable Player award. Caminiti died in 2004 at age forty-one. Experts say steroids may have contributed to his poor health.

Top athletes are role models for teenagers. When their sports heroes say they used steroids to boost their performance, many high school athletes think steroids will help them too. In 2007, 2 percent of American high school students said that they had used steroids at least once in their life. But anabolic steroids are especially unhealthy for teenagers.

CHAPTER TWO

HEALTH DANGERS

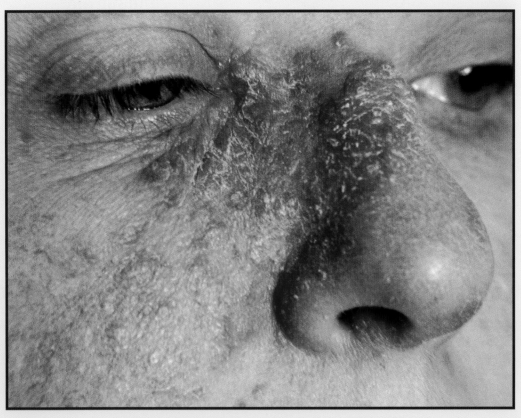

A steroid user shows one tell-tale sign of steroid use, Rosacea.

Steroids come in many forms. Some are rubbed on the skin. Others are injected or swallowed. All forms are bad for your health. All steroids have harmful side effects, both short term and long term.

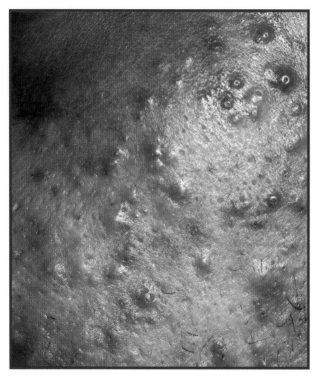

Steroid users often experience nasty acne outbreaks.

Some steroid users get headaches and muscle **cramps** soon after taking the drug. Others may feel dizzy. One of the best-known signs of steroid use is bad **acne**. Acne can show up within weeks of using steroids. It can leave permanent scars. Some male steroid users grow lots of hair on the face and body. Female users also grow thicker facial hair. At the same time, hair can fall out from the top of the head. This can lead to early baldness in both men and women. Other effects include bad body odors, red or purple spots on the skin, and trembling.

With continued abuse, the physical side effects get more serious. Studies have shown that anabolic steroids can cause liver and kidney tumors. They can also lead to high blood pressure and an enlarged heart. Males who use steroids may develop breasts. Females' voices may deepen. Steroids can damage the reproductive organs in both males and females.

Teenagers who take steroids run even more risks. For instance, the drugs make the skeleton stop growing. Teens may stay the same height for the rest of their lives. Teens are more likely to mix different kinds of steroids and take them nonstop. This raises the risk of harm.

A lot of information about steroids can be found on the Internet. Some Web sites are from anti-steroids organizations. Other Web sites are from health organizations. These sites usually talk about the legal and health dangers of steroids. Other Web sites that seem informative are really just steroid dealers. These sites illegally sell drugs, but they also talk about health. They say that taking steroids is no big deal. How can you tell good information from bad on the Internet? Consider who is providing the information. What is their background? Also, think about their goal. Do they want to sell a product?

A steroid user can experience mood swings, depression, and worry.

Using steroids can change the personality as well. Many steroid users become nervous and **paranoid**. They can be high-strung and angry one day, depressed the next. Experts think steroids can make people violent. In 2006, Greek researchers took identical twins from the same town and with the same diet. They gave steroids to one twin in each pair. The twin on steroids was more aggressive and paranoid than the twin not on steroids.

In spite of all these known side effects, athletes around the world risk their health and their careers by taking steroids.

Can you tell if someone you know takes steroids? In addition to getting bigger and stronger, some steroid users show:

- sudden increase in acne
- angry, paranoid behavior
- new, thicker hair on the face
- yellow tint to the skin and eyes
- increased nervousness.

It is important to know that nobody shows all the signs and that people can show signs without using steroids. Many teenagers get acne, and most boys start growing hair on their faces in their teens.

CHAPTER THREE

STEROIDS IN SPORTS

*Olympic athlete Marion Jones was stripped of
her medals after admitting steroid use.*

Marion Jones was one of the most famous female
athletes in the world in 2000. The American track and
field star won three gold medals and two bronze medals
at the Sydney Olympics that year. In 2007, Jones admitted

that she took steroids before the 2000 Olympics. She was suspended from athletics. She lost her medals. And because she lied about steroids to federal agents, she went to jail.

Steroids have ruined the sports careers of many famous athletes. Their stories often follow a similar plot. The athletes set an amazing record or start a new season in far better shape than ever before. They get far better scores than ever before too. The athletes are honored for their achievements. And then they're disgraced when they're exposed as steroid users. The athletes are punished and usually the record is erased. As long as steroid use is against the rules,

In 1988, Canadian Ben Johnson was called the fastest man on earth. He won an Olympic gold medal and broke the world record in the 100-meter dash. A few days later, Johnson tested positive for steroids. He was labeled a cheater. His gold medal was taken away and his career was over. Was this the right response? What do you think should happen to athletes when they get caught taking steroids? Why do you think this?

Olympic runner Ben Johnson set a world record in the100-meter dash. He also admitted to using steroids. Olympic athletes say the games are rife with steroid users.

athletic achievement is supposed to come from skill, training, and effort. It is not supposed to come from drugs that boost performance.

Steroid use is also called "doping" or "juicing." And it's often very hard to prove. Historically, steroid use has been more common in sports that depend on size and strength. These include sports such as weight lifting, track and field, baseball, cycling, and football.

Controversy over steroid use often takes place in the sport of cycling. That sport's most famous race is the annual Tour de France. The race is so long that it takes 20 stages over three weeks. At stage 17 of the 2006 race, American Floyd Landis came from behind. He stunned the cycling world with a very fast solo ride. Three days later he won the Tour. It soon came out, however, that he had tested positive for steroids the day he had his great ride. He said he was innocent. But his title was taken from him. The doping scandal ruined his reputation.

Steroid use has also been a problem in Major League Baseball. In the 1990s, home run records that had stood for decades were being broken every year. Many people suspect that the best sluggers—including Mark McGwire,

21st Century Content

The NCAA is a sports organization of American colleges and universities. It oversees thousands of student athletes. The NCAA tests more than 10,000 student athletes each year for steroids and other drugs. If an athlete tests positive, he or she is suspended for the year. Many colleges and universities have their own testing policies and harsher penalties. Go online to find out more about the NCAA's drug-testing policies. Then find out about the testing policies of another sports organization; for example, the one that runs the Olympics. How do these policies differ? How are they the same? Does one group's policy seem more effective than the other's?

Winner of the 2007 Tour de France, Floyd Landis was found to have an elevated amount of testosterone in his blood, leading officials to claim he used steroids. Landis has repeatedly claimed he was falsely accused.

Sammy Sosa, and Barry Bonds—could not get that much stronger unless they were using steroids. Most players deny using steroids. Some players, however, have accused their former teammates of taking steroids. Fans cannot be sure. Many still wonder about the top ballplayers.

Athletes have been using steroids for years. And they have been getting caught for years too. Steroid makers and users find new ways to disguise drug use. Official agencies find better testing methods. And the controversy continues.

CHAPTER FOUR

STOPPING STEROID USE

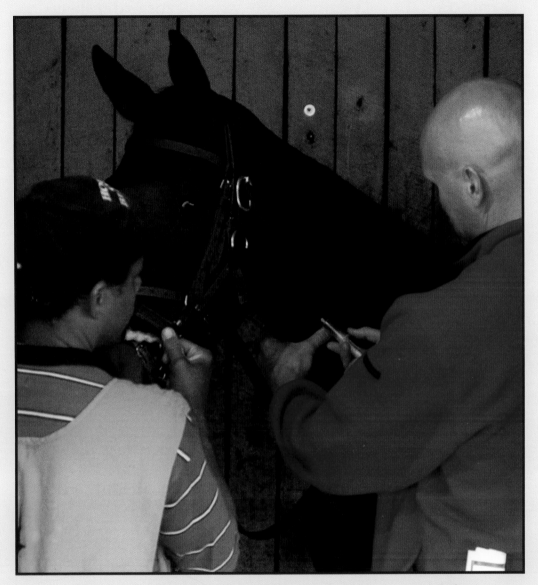

A state veterinarian takes a blood sample from race horse Sister Bay before a race at Churchill Downs. The entrants in horse races are among the most closely monitored athletes in the world, part of an initiative to crack down on the use of anabolic steroids and other performance-enhancing drugs.

Many people work very hard to keep sports and society free of illegal steroid use. Some of these people work for the government. Other people work for anti-drug agencies. And some work for sports leagues and teams.

Steroids are not legal in the United States, Canada, and many other countries unless a doctor prescribes them for a medical problem. In the United States, it is illegal to buy, sell, or have steroids that aren't for legal personal use. It is illegal to buy or sell steroids in Canada. In both countries, people can go to prison for breaking steroid laws. Police and drug agents track down steroid dealers and buyers to stop the flow of drugs.

The World Anti-Doping Agency (WADA) was created in 1999. Its goal is to stop the use of steroids in sports. WADA works with countries around the world to educate and test athletes.

WADA, the World Anti-Doping Agency, was founded in 1991. Pictured are 2008 president John Fahey (right), with David Howman, the director general.

Many sports leagues and organizations use WADA's list of banned substances. All forms of anabolic steroids are on that list.

Sports leagues are one of the most important groups working to make athletics steroid-free. Without enforcement, more athletes would be tempted to take steroids.

Olympic athlete Zach Lund was issued a public warning by the U.S. Anti-Doping Agency after he tested positive at the World Cup for Finasteride, a banned substance often used as a steroid-masking agent.

The International Olympic Committee takes a tough stance on steroids. Olympic athletes are tested for steroids. If more than an allowable amount is found in the athlete's blood or urine, he or she is banned from competition. The athlete also loses any medals won. More than 20 athletes had problems with steroids and other banned substances during the 2004 Olympics. Some of them did not show up for drug tests. Others tested positive and were disqualified. They were also kicked out of the Olympics.

The National Football League is also hard on steroid users. The NFL tests players all season long. If a player tests positive, he is suspended without pay. For some players, that means losing millions of dollars.

So you can see that several groups work toward the same goal. They all try to keep athletes from using steroids.

Today, major sports organizations use high-tech testing to find steroid users. They take samples of an athlete's urine or blood. They use computers and lab equipment to search for and measure steroids and other banned substances. But sometimes the tests have errors. Some athletes have been accused publicly of taking steroids or some other banned substance but were later cleared. How can sports groups prevent this from happening? Should test results be made public? And if so, when?

CHAPTER FIVE

STAYING CLEAR OF STEROIDS

Ryan O'Sullivan was one of three high school students facing steroids charges in New Haven, Connecticut. Even high school students take steroids to improve performance.

Taylor Hooten was a high school baseball player in Plano, Texas. His coach told him he needed to be bigger. So he began taking anabolic steroids to bulk up. When his parents learned that he was taking steroids, Taylor promised to stop. Shortly after that, he became depressed. Then in July 2003 he committed **suicide**. He was 17. His parents and others think that his depression and suicide were caused by the steroids. They helped to get a new law passed in Texas. It requires testing high school athletes for steroids.

In Texas, New Jersey, and parts of New Mexico, high school athletes are randomly tested for steroids. Other states may soon do the same. Many other states

High schools around the country have different policies on steroid use. Some suspend athletes found to be using steroids. Others require counseling or detention. In some schools, steroid use can get an athlete kicked out of his or her sport. Find out what the high school nearest you says about steroid use among athletes. What are the testing policies? What are the penalties?

The Washington Redskins announce that they have joined the NFL's ATLAS and ATHENA Drug Prevention programs to combat the use of steroids and human growth hormone at the high school level.

have laws relating to high school athletes and steroid use. Some of these laws call for punishment or drug education if students are found to be taking steroids. Usually, the students are kicked out of the sports program. Often, they also get in trouble with their school. Sometimes a young person who tests positive for steroids is sent to in-school suspension or detention. Usually, he or she must go to drug counseling.

High schools in California started a new program after teenagers there also committed suicide after taking steroids. The program trains and educates coaches about the dangers of steroids. It also teaches people how to spot steroid use. And it educates athletes and their parents and makes them sign a promise not to use steroids.

Educational programs are designed to teach athletes and their families about the dangers of steroid use. Because many young people hear stories about famous athletes

Assistant director of New Jersey State Interscholastic Athletic Association Bob Baly announced that New Jersey had become the first state to institute a statewide steroid-testing policy for high school athletes.

doing steroids, they think it might be OK to take steroids too. They don't know enough about the bad things that can happen to them if they take steroids. These programs tell athletes that steroids are illegal. They tell them that people go to jail for using steroids. And they say that they can be very bad for a person's health.

Steroids are dangerous drugs. They can be especially harmful to young people. Many people try to make sure that teenagers and children do not use them. But the best way to prevent steroid use is to teach young people about their harmful effects so they will choose to play sports without drug use.

Learning & Innovation Skills

Think of a situation where a coach or teammate urges you to take steroids so that you become better at a sport. There would be a lot of pressure to make the right decision. What would you say? How would you make a good decision?

Glossary

acne (AK-nee) pimples or cysts, especially on the face, that can leave permanent scars

anabolic (AN-uh-BALL-ik) a chemical process that builds tissue in the body

anabolic steroids human-made chemicals that work like male hormones to increase muscle growth and strength

controversy (KON-truh-VER-see) an issue over which people strongly disagree

cramps sudden, painful, and involuntary tightening of a muscle

disqualified (dis-KWOL-uh-fide) barred from or kicked out of competition

paranoid (PARE-uh-noyd) overly suspicious and distrustful of other people

reputation (rep-yoo-TAY-shun) the quality of a person's character, as judged by others

suicide (SOO-ih-side) the act of killing oneself on purpose

FOR MORE INFORMATION

Books

Connolly, Sean. *Steroids*. Just the Facts. Chicago: Heinemann Library, 2000.

Fitzhugh, Karla. *Steroids*. Chicago: Raintree, 2003.

Monroe, Judy. *Steroids, Sports, and Body Image: The Risks of Performance-Enhancing Drugs*. Issues in Focus. Berkeley Heights, NJ: Enslow, 2004.

Spring, Albert. *Steroids and Your Muscles: The Incredibly Disgusting Story*. Incredibly Disgusting Drugs. New York: Rosen Central, 2001.

Web Sites

"Anabolic Steroids," Facts on Drugs, NIDA for Teens
http://teens.drugabuse.gov/facts/facts_ster1.asp
Information for kids about steroids from the U.S. government

"Steroids," KidsHealth
www.kidshealth.org/kid/stay_healthy/fit/steroids.html
KidsHealth looks at the risks of steroids for kids

TeenHealthFX
www.teenhealthfx.com/answers/Sports/subcategory.php?subsection=74
TeenHealthFX answers questions about steroids and other performance-enhancing drugs

INDEX

ABOUT THE AUTHOR

A.R. Schaefer has written many books for children. He likes sports and being outdoors.